DOWN IN THE DUMPS

TRASH VS. TRUCKS

ALSO BY WES HARGIS:

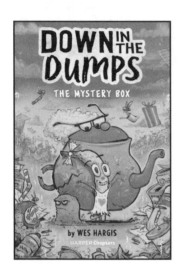

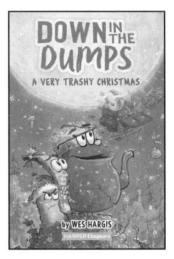

Read more
Down in the Dumps
books!

HARPER Chapters

DOWN IN THE DUMPS

TRASH VS. TRUCKS

WES HARGIS

HARPER
An Imprint of HarperCollins*Publishers*

For my mom, Bobby Hargis

Down in the Dumps #2: Trash vs. Trucks

Library of Congress Control Number: 2021031449
ISBN 978-0-06-291015-8 — ISBN 978-0-06-291016-5 (paperback)

Typography by Torborg Davern
22 23 24 25 26   PC/LSCC   10 9 8 7 6 5 4 3 2 1
❖
First Edition

CONTENTS

CHAPTER 1
IT'S THE END

It was a beautiful morning at the Gunderson Farm . . .

That is, until a line of green stench crossed under the nose of Farmer Gunderson and his dog.

WESTERFIELD WASTE TRANSFER AND RECYCLING CENTER

The stench, as always, was coming across the river, from the Westerfield Dump.

It was Tuesday. This meant Ms. Kettle was cooking muck pies.

The Zoop Loop nearby shot out slime that sounded like an emptying ketchup bottle.

GLORP

POOF

NANA!
MORELAND!
Breakfast!

Oh,
fiddlesticks.

Moreland was relaxing in his ooze pond. He was blowing snot bubbles of different sizes.

Nana was reading a newspaper that had just blown in.

CHAPTER 2
HERE THEY COME!

Stop, stop, stop! There's been a mistake!

A BIG MISTAKE!

They scrambled over to the billboard.

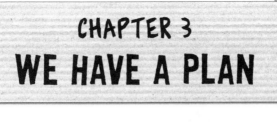

CHAPTER 3
WE HAVE A PLAN

Nana had a plan. It started with asking for help from critters she didn't even like very much.

WHAT, WHO, WHOOZIT?

Get up, Mungles!

KICK

TUNA

16

17

Just then a thunderous *CRACK!* echoed across the canyon . . .

Two gigantic bulldozers scooped up the entire Old Fridge Hill right in front of them.

They dumped the piles onto the waiting barge in the Yamapol River.

CHAPTER 4
RETREAT!

The next morning there was trash running everywhere.

26

CRUNCH

At that point, Nana had had enough.

Then all the dozers and trucks drove off for the day.

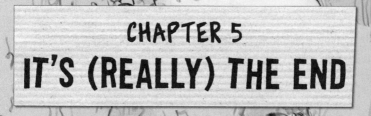

CHAPTER 5
IT'S (REALLY) THE END

Ms. K spent the late evening packing all her spices and cooking tins.

Nana started saying goodbye to all her favorite spots.

And then she moped for a bit.

Bye, Trash Canyon.

Nana smelled smoke in the distance and peered over to see what looked like a flickering light.

Nana and Moreland wandered along the ridge of The Trash Canyon toward the light and peered down over the edge.

It's the trucks and the yellow city dozers!

The dozers and trucks were snoring loudly, except for two. They were quietly talking next to the glowing campfire.

While Nana was hanging there, she had wanted to tell them to just get up and *leave* if they didn't like the dump . . .

CHAPTER 6
THE TRASHTACULAR

The next morning Nana pulled out her bucket of black slime paint and wandered over to a broken white door.

As Nana painted, trash stopped running in a panic and began to surround her.

When she finished, Nana walked her painting over to the very center of the dump, next to the old fridge.

That morning Nana called friends from three nearby county dumps to spread the word about the Trashtacular.

Come live here!

We've got the best smells, the biggest bugs, and all the muck!

It wasn't long before trash started coming in from everywhere.

It would blow in from the east and then a bunch more would come from the south . . .

. . . and then the southwest.

Ms. K was busy cooking goo biscuits for the new trash as Nana tallied up the numbers.

10,007 . . . 10,008, 10,009 pieces . . .

That's a lot of trash!

Maybe. But is it enough?

Nana had an idea to find out just how much trash was there.

Okay, everyone! Group picture!

Nana pulled out her flip phone to take a photo and . . .

Okay, tall trash in the back.

Everyone gather around the big sign.

WESTERFIELD DUMP TRASHTACULAR!
COME FOR THE PARTY...
STAY FOR THE BEAUTY
COME LIVE IN WESTERFIELD

54

CHAPTER 8
TO THE CITY!

The three of them had to hurry. The trucks were already leaving.

There goes the last one now!

Nana and her friends waited for the truck to drive by.

Everybody drop!

THUD!

59

It was a pleasant ride to Westerfield. The truck talked the whole way about where all his trash pickups were in town.

This is our stop, then! Thanks, Mr. Truck!

They stopped and spoke to the trash in the West Side trash piles.

The mall trash bins . . .

The downtown cans . . .

61

Roadside trash no one seems to pick up . . .

The field trash in between the big box stores . . .

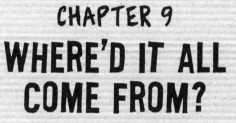

CHAPTER 9
WHERE'D IT ALL COME FROM?

The next morning Nana, Ms. Kettle, and Moreland all slept in. No one woke when the trucks came in.

The trucks were being hit by a strange deluge of debris from the sky above.

Freeland, the bent straw, knocked furiously on the microwave door.

Nana! Ms. Kettle! You have to see this!

Just then a wave of new, goopy trash toppled over and . . .

SPLOOOSH!

. . . covered the dozers. It shot the gang high into the air.

The dozers brought back every last piece of trash from the barge.

And Nana, Ms. K, and Moreland sat on top of the old pole and ate muck pies while they watched.

That old fan goes over there! Thank you!

Then they all watched happily as the city dozers drove away.

The dump was back to normal and better than ever. The piles were even higher and the stink was . . .

Sniff. Not bad at all. What do you think, Moreland?

Meh.

Nana spent the day welcoming the new trash and finding each a place to settle.

Nana told Big Bettie the whole story as they settled back into life at the dump.

And it was perfect.

Now that all the garbage was where it belonged, the town of Westerfield was cleaner than ever.

CONGRATULATIONS!

You've read **11** chapters,

87 pages,

and **1,705** words!

All your help paid off!

SUPER SMELLY FUN

THINK

Nana, Mrs. Kettle, and Moreland travel all around town to find more trash to bring to the Westerfield Dump. Draw a map of your hometown and mark all the places that you like to visit.

FEEL

To save her home, Nana creates an invitation for all the trash in town to move to the dump. Imagine you're having a party and inviting all your friends over. Create your own invitation to tell them about the fun you've planned.

ACT

Moreland doesn't want to be forced out of his home at the

dump. But sometimes going someplace new can be fun. Write a story about moving to someplace new. It can be anywhere! Describe all the fun, amazing new things you discover.

WES HARGIS is an author-illustrator living in the desert of Arizona. He began his career in the Tucson newspaper industry and honed his craft late at night while landscaping in the hot sun during the day. The first children's book he ever illustrated was *Jackson and Bud's Bumpy Ride*. Since then, Wes has worked on lots of books, including *When I Grow Up* (a *New York Times* bestseller!) by "Weird Al" Yankovic and the Let's Investigate with Nate science series by Nate Ball.

Wes likes to draw on scratchy paper, but these days he mostly uses a big tablet. Wes loves hanging out with his kids and exploring the desert. He also loves making his own Mexican food and the color yellow-green (like Moreland).

He's married to his lovely wife, Debbie. They have three opinionated kids, two evil cats, and one happily clueless dog. And plants. Lots of plants.